P9-CFM-299

This book is dedicated with love
to the miracles in my life . . .
my wondrous sons, Billy, Nik, and Ethan

CHALK

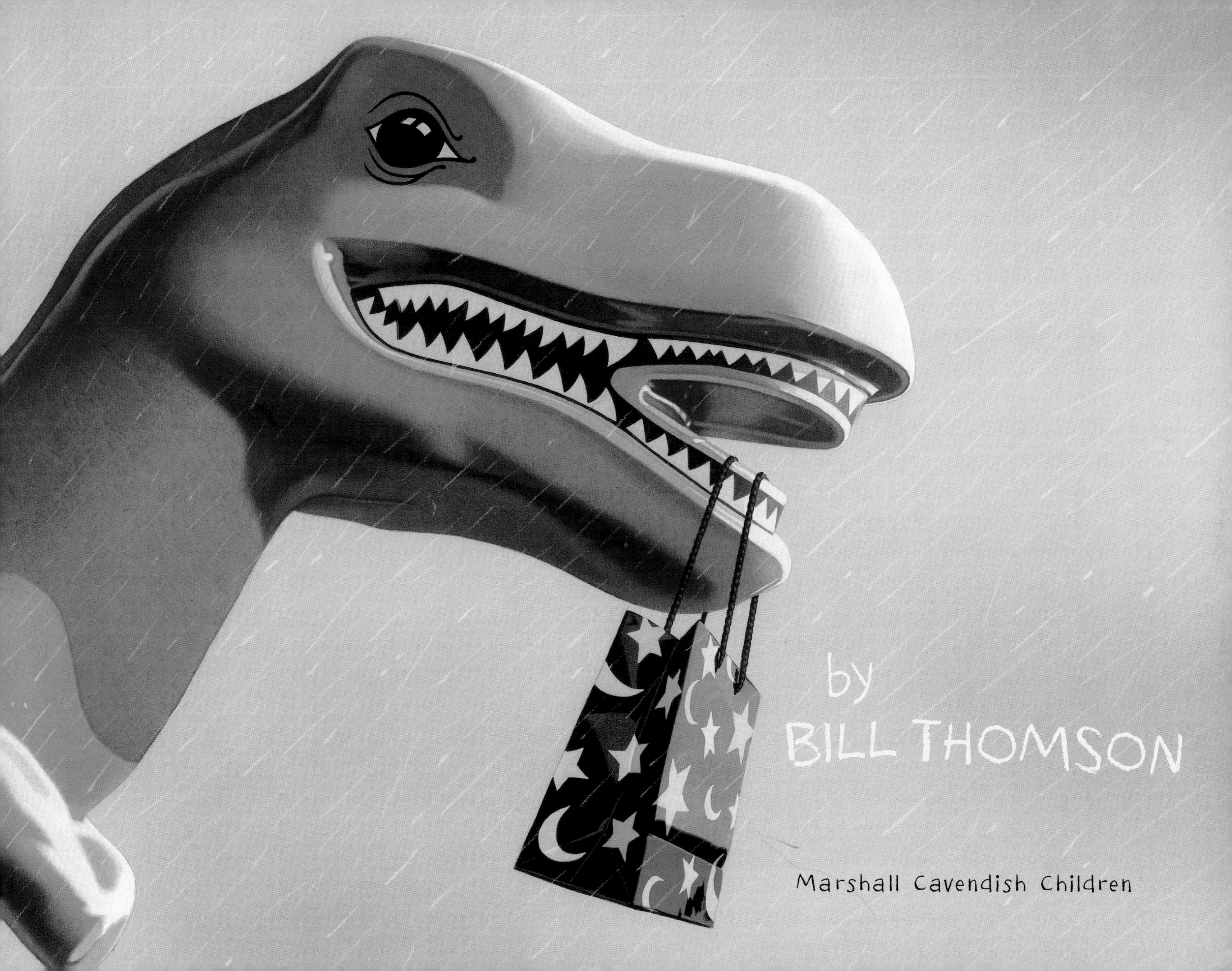

by
BILL THOMSON

Marshall Cavendish Children

Marshall Cavendish Corporation, 99 White Plains Road, Tarrytown, NY 10591
www.marshallcavendish.us/kids
LIBRARY OF CONGRESS CATALOGING-IN-PUBLICATION DATA:
Thomson, Bill, 1963-
Chalk / illustrated by Bill Thomson.—1st ed.
p. cm.
Summary: A wordless picture book about three children who go to a park on a rainy day, find some chalk, and draw pictures that come to life.
ISBN 978-0-7614-5526-4
[1. Drawing--Fiction. 2. Stories without words.] I. Title.
PZ7.T37383Ch 2010
[E]—dc22
2009014141
Bill Thomson embraced traditional painting techniques and meticulously painted each illustration by hand, using acrylic paint and colored pencils. His illustrations are not photographs or computer generated images.
Book design by Michael Nelson Editor: Margery Cuyler
Printed in China (E)
First edition
6
Marshall Cavendish Children

Bill Thomson would like to give special thanks to GameTime for use of their extraordinary Dinosaur Adventure Mates playground ride. He would also like to thank Margery Cuyler and Anahid Hamparian for making a dream come true.